This book should be returned to any branch of the
Lancashire County Library on or before the date shown

Lancashire County Library,
County Hall Complex,
1st floor Christ Church Precinct,
Preston, PR1 8XJ

www.lancashire.gov.uk/libraries

LL1(A)

In loving memory of my uncle Michael.

First published in the UK in 2017
by New Frontier Publishing (Europe) Pty. Ltd.
93 Harbord Street, London SW6 6PN
www.newfrontierpublishing.co.uk

ISBN: 978-1-912076-71-0

Text copyright © Candice Lemon-Scott 2014
Illustrations copyright © New Frontier Publishing 2014
Illustrations by Celeste Hulme
The rights of Candice Lemon-Scott to be identified as the author and Celeste
Hulme to be identified as the illustrator of this work have been asserted.

A CIP catalogue record for this book is available from the British Library.

Printed in China
10 9 8 7 6 5 4 3 2 1

Cover illustration and design by Celeste Hulme

JAKE IN SPACE
ROCKET BATTLES

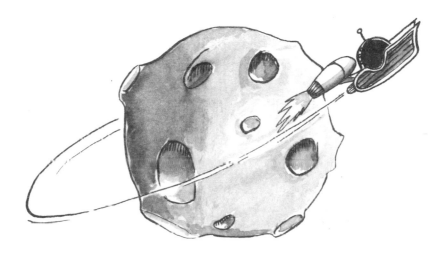

Candice Lemon-Scott
Illustrated by Celeste Hulme

Bright lights flashed in Jake's eyes. Squinting, he looked over at his friends Milly, Skye and Rory. They looked as stunned as he felt. There were people everywhere, hoping to catch a glimpse of the Rocket Battles racing stars. A reporter shoved a giant microphone in front of Jake's face.

'Jack, leader of the Blazing Comets race team ...' the reporter began.

'It's Jake,' he said, hearing his voice booming

around the crowded hangar.

'Okay, Jayyyyyyke. How does it feel to lead the youngest team ever to race in the Rocket Battles?'

'Um … ah, scary?'

Skye leaned in. 'And exciting. We're *very* excited to be here,' she added.

Jake smiled, glad Skye had saved him from sounding silly. It had been only a year since he had met Skye, Rory and Milly at the Remedial Space Car Driving School. There, they had finally got their space car driving licences – and had quickly become the best of friends. Now they were about to race in the biggest and best space car race in the whole solar system. Although the race was incredibly dangerous, it was every kid's dream to race in it.

The reporter moved onto the next team. They were dressed in slick red suits. Jake knew straightaway these racers were the

Mars Misfits, even though he'd never seen them in real life before. Only the top teams were chosen for the Rocket Battles, and the Mars Misfits were so good they always made it into the race. For the past five years they had won. Their suits all had 'Solar System Design' in large letters on the front – this was the company that gave the team money to race and created their space cars. Jake could hardly believe he was going to be racing them.

The Misfits waved at the crowd, and they cheered and whistled back. Jake could only imagine how exciting it would be to be that popular.

The leader of the Misfits stepped forward with a toothy grin. His team's car gleamed beside him as he tapped the fresh paintwork of the sleek entry hatch. A couple of teenage girls at the front almost fainted. One girl even had to take a sip of OX POWER, an energy drink with extra oxygen that was often used in low-gravity fields. It was also handy for screaming fans who got so excited they forgot to breathe.

'Matt, as leader of the Misfits, why don't you tell us what you have planned for the race this year?'

'Now that would be telling,' Matt said, winking. 'When we win I'll let you in on a few of our secrets. How does that sound?'

The reporter giggled like a little girl. 'Okay! Good luck – not that you'll need it.'

The Misfits waved again and the crowd cheered even louder.

Away from the microphone, Matt turned, looked straight at Jake and hissed, 'Unlike some other teams, we *deserve* our place in the race.'

Jake turned as red as Matt's suit. Every year one team was chosen as a wildcard entry. This

4

year it was Jake's team – the Blazing Comets.

'Would you listen to him?' Rory said, frowning. 'I think saving the Earth and the Moon is a good enough reason to be chosen for the race.'

Jake couldn't help but grin. It was amazing to think a bunch of remedial kids had stopped the evil Gradock from blowing up the planet. The Central Intergalactic Agency (CIA) had chosen them as the wildcard entry because of the driving skills they had used in stopping Gradock.

'Don't worry about him,' Milly added. 'We can do this.'

Jake wasn't so sure they were ready. After all, they hadn't had their normal driving licences for long, and now they were going to race a super-performance car with mega rocket boosters! Plus, the Rocket Battles race was brutal. The only rule was that the team whose members made it across the finish line first was the winner. Even if only one team member made it back.

The reporter moved onto the next team, who were dressed in purple. Everyone knew the Neptune Goons had been coming in at a disappointing second place since the Misfits came along. Before the Mars team had started racing, the Goons had won twelve races in a row. But now they had lost all their sponsors. It showed in their scruffy, worn suits and the dull-looking car beside them.

'It's many years since you were the champions, Blake,' the reporter said to the team leader, grimly. 'Do you think you'll ever regain your place as victors, or is it too late for the Goons?'

'Watch and see. This is the year we'll have a comeback and everyone will know who the true champions are again,' Blake answered.

'And what if you lose again? Will you retire?'

'We *won't* lose,' Blake replied.

'Spoken like true racers. Give it up for the Goons!' the reporter yelled.

The crowd gave a small, polite clap.

Jake took a deep breath and turned up the volume on the communication controls. He hadn't felt this nervous since he went for his space car licence. He was just glad he had his good friends with him.

A computerised voice crackled through the car's speakers. 'The Rocket Battles will begin in ten minutes. Please finish all space car checks.'

'Ten minutes! We only have ten minutes,' Milly cried.

Milly was in charge of systems operations. Even though she'd been studying hard, she still found it hard to remember all the different parts. The race cars were much more complicated than normal space cars. She hurried to recheck all the signals and lights, her hands shaking. Jake realised he wasn't the only one who was feeling nervous.

Jake positioned himself for his job of forward navigation, buckling himself into the front seat. Skye sat in the back in her role as rear navigator.

'Two minutes to go,' Rory said.

Milly switched on the controls. Just as Rory was about to take his place in the driver's seat, the lower hatch opened. To Jake's surprise, Henry's head appeared. He pulled himself up and flopped onto the floor. A silver drill was poking out of his forearm. He pressed the drill against his arm and closed his skin over the top.

'All mechanical checks and updates are now complete.' He pulled down his shirt sleeve and

gave his arm a tap.

'Henry!' Jake smiled. It was still pretty cool knowing a real cyborg. Henry worked for the CIA and he was the one who had alerted Jake that something strange was going on at the remedial driving school. They had all become friends too – though Rory never seemed too happy to see him.

'What are you doing here?' Rory growled at Henry.

'I have been sent,' Henry replied.

'What's that supposed to mean?' Rory huffed. Before Henry could say any more there was another announcement.

'The race is about to begin. Please fasten your seatbelts and prepare for take-off.'

Henry put himself in the driver's seat and buckled himself in.

'Hey, that's my spot!' Rory exclaimed.

'The CIA has granted me role of driver. You

are second-in-command,' Henry said matter-of-factly.

'You're driving? Are you *serious*?' Rory cried.

'He *is* just about the best driver in the entire universe,' Skye said.

'Have you forgotten that he nearly crashed us into the side of the Remedial Space Car Driving School last year?' Rory replied.

'You know that was just to cover up that he was really working for the CIA,' Milly reminded him.

Rory looked at Jake, but Jake knew the girls were right. The other teams were going to be almost impossible to beat. If they had any chance of winning this race it would be with Henry driving. Being the CIA's cyborg, he was the best of the best.

'Start your engines,' the computer announced.

'You'd better buckle up,' Jake said to Rory.

Rory sighed and sat down beside Henry. Jake brought up the forward projection screen while Skye brought up the rear one. There was a huge floating barrier in front of the racers. The cars were lined up, their bumpers almost touching the barrier. Jake panned the viewer around. Through the screen he could see the green car of the Pluto Pilgrims, the blue car of the Earth Avengers and the purple car of the Neptune Goons. The Blazing Comets' yellow car was on the end. It was the super-performance race car they had been training in, and the CIA had loaned it to them for the race.

All the cars were specially designed for racing. They were narrow at the front for speed and wider at the back where the rocket boosters were. In this race the teams would have to zoom through the entire solar system, so their cars used only the fastest technology and the most modern designs. Jake could hear the engines humming and revving. It was starting to feel like space bugs were doing cartwheels in his stomach.

Skye brought up the rear projection screen. They all crowded around to look as the second row of battle cars appeared. There was the orange car of the Saturn Speedsters and the brown car belonging to the Venus Victors. Right behind them was the bright red car that belonged to the infamous Mars Misfits. The grille on the front of it gleamed like a silvery sneer. Jake shuddered as the car's lights flashed amber and then red.

There was another announcement, 'Your clue for checkpoint one is: Near side, far side. You can't always see me but I'm always here.'

They all laughed. That one was easy. 'We're going to the Moon first!' Milly laughed.

Jake couldn't believe their first stop would be the place where the friends first met. *It's lucky that Gradock is safely locked away in prison now*, Jake thought.

'On your marks. Get set. GO!'

The barrier disappeared and the race began.

'Mega rocket boosters engaged,' Milly called.

They all knew they were going to need a lot of speed to escape the Earth's atmosphere and get into orbit. But before they had even lifted off, a flash of red sped across the forward projection screen. The Blazing Comets all gasped at the same time.

'Did you see that? How are we ever going to beat the Mars Misfits?' Rory sighed.

'That is the attitude of a space race loser, my friend,' Henry said.

'Who are you calling a loser?' Rory yelled.

But Jake thought Rory was right. How could a bunch of remedial space car drivers ever beat the best racers in the entire solar system? They just had to focus on one thing – finishing the race in one piece.

Jake looked at the screen. He could see that the purple, green and blue cars were already just spots of colour in the distance. Then a blur of orange and brown passed the screen and disappeared.

'We'd better get a move on, and fast,' he said.

Five heads were pressed back against the seats as the rocket boosters were launched. The Blazing Comets' car shot into the atmosphere and quickly into orbit. As they gained even more speed, Milly set a course towards the Moon and their car accelerated out of the atmosphere and into the darkness of space. Jake felt like he was floating on a bed of marshmallows as they hit zero gravity. Even though they were moving at the speed of a rocket, it felt as if they were cruising along gently. Henry's expert driving helped as he directed them to the Moon.

Jake had missed this feeling since returning from remedial school. Back on Earth's space station, where he lived, gravity was controlled. But one thing he didn't miss was the mess of hair now on top of his head. His hair was normally boofy but in zero gravity it turned into a wild frizzball. When he looked back he saw that Skye was staring at him with a grin on her face. Now he was *sure* he didn't miss the zero-gravity hair problem. He looked at Henry. As always, his black hair was sitting perfectly flat against his head.

'Do you have any of that no-gravity hair wax, Henry?' Jake asked.

The cyborg smiled and pulled a small jar from his pocket. It glowed fluoro pink and the wax throbbed inside the glass container. He handed it to Jake.

'Are you sure this is the stuff?' Jake said.

'Yes. It is a new, improved version. Just dab a tiny amount onto your finger and rub it in. It is marvellous. I find it to be one of the perks of working for the CIA.'

Jake opened the jar and sniffed. He nearly threw up. The stuff *stank*. It was worse than the time he left bean stew in his lunchbox and forgot about it for two months.

'Yuck! Put that away,' Rory cried, pinching his nostrils closed.

'There's no way I'm putting that on my head,' Jake said, passing the wax back to Henry.

'True, it is a bit on the nose, as you say,'

Henry agreed. 'A tiny amount will not cause any problems with smell, however.'

'Easy for you to say – you probably don't even smell,' Rory said.

'Actually, I have all six senses,' Henry claimed.

'Six?' Milly said. 'There are only five senses.'

'You humans always forget the most important one of all,' Henry argued. 'Instinct.'

'Only mums have that,' Skye said.

'That is because mothers are the only people who bother to use it. Having children activates the lost sense.'

Jake turned again to see Skye was still staring at his crazy brown mass of hair. It had become even fuzzier as they travelled deeper into space. He dabbed the tiniest bit of wax on his finger and rubbed it into his hair. Within moments his hair flattened smoothly against his head. That was better. Skye smiled at him and he grinned back.

Bang!

Jake jerked forward. The jar of no-gravity hair wax flew from his hand, and when he looked up he saw that it was almost empty. Most of the wax had escaped, and bright pink glowing blobs floated around the car. Jake quickly grabbed as much of the floating wax as he could, trapped it in the jar and stuffed it in his suit pocket.

'What just happened?' Milly cried.

Jake couldn't see anything besides stars in the forward screen.

'Bring up the rear screen,' Jake said.

Skye brought up the screen.

'There's something red streaking across the stars,' she said. 'Wait! It's doubling back.'

It looked as though the Mars Misfits were already up to no good, Jake thought. He looked in the forward screen again. He still couldn't see anything.

Bang!

This time they were thrown sideways.

'What is going on?' Rory shouted.

'It's the Misfits,' Skye said. 'They must be trying to throw us off course.'

Bang!

This time they were thrown sideways in the other direction.

'What are we going to do?' Milly screamed.

'I have an idea,' Henry said. 'Hold onto your seats.'

'And your noses,' Rory added, trying to avoid the dollops of wax still floating around.

Henry moved the car into a vertical position.

'Set the controls for full power, Rory,' he commanded.

'What are you doing?' Jake asked.

'We will shoot straight to the Moon at full speed,' Henry replied.

'We can't come in that fast!' Rory argued.

'I don't think we have any other choice,' Jake said. Unless they wanted to be turned into a squashed turnip by the Misfits before they even reached the first checkpoint. But it was going to be a rough Moon landing, heading there at such high speed.

Henry insisted Milly enter the command code. She hit the final button and the car shot up, pushing everyone back against their seats, even against zero gravity. With the force, the last blobs of hair wax splattered all over the crew.

'Ewwww!' Milly screamed.

'Ahhhh!' Skye cried.

'Yuck!' Jake exclaimed.

Rory held his breath. Only Henry seemed unworried.

'I thought you said you could smell,' Rory complained between clenched teeth.

'I can. But I can also switch my senses off,' Henry said. 'One of the good things about being a cyborg.'

Rory looked like he was about to strangle Henry but the speed of the car held him back in his seat. Jake was concentrating on the forward screen when he saw a shower of sparks rain down on the nose of their car.

'Sparks!' he shouted. 'What's happening behind us, Skye?' he said.

She panned the rear viewfinder down and gasped. 'You'd better take a look at this!'

They twisted as far as they could in their seats towards the rear projection screen and watched as the Misfits rammed the Venus Victors. The brown car spun off course and hurtled back towards Earth, out of control. They were out of the race.

'Wow – that could have been us,' Milly gulped.

Seeing the red car looping back around towards them, Skye cried, 'We're not safe yet!'

Henry accelerated even more and the Blazing Comets shot away.

With the Misfits out of sight again, Jake watched as the round disc of the Moon became larger and larger on the forward projection screen.

'Get ready for a crash landing,' he yelled.

As they rapidly came closer, Jake could see the shapes of the Moon's craters. Soon the grey block of the old Remedial Space Car Driving School came into view. That building still sent a shiver down his spine – like someone had

put cold spaghetti down his back – and he remembered Gradock and his evil plan. The building was mostly empty now, but as they sped closer Jake saw lights hovering above it, which meant that it was their first checkpoint. But there was no more time to think as they approached the building – fast.

'Not a Moon crash landing again,' Rory cried.

Rory wasn't the only one remembering how Henry had crash-landed last time they were on the Moon.

'This time I have prepared for such an event,' Henry said calmly. 'Milly, you'll notice a small orange button to your left. Please push it.'

Milly pressed the button before covering her face for impact.

Jake heard a whooshing sound and the car slowed so suddenly it felt like they'd actually reversed. The building was still getting closer, only a lot more slowly. How was that happening?

'Check this out,' Skye said, pointing at her screen.

Jake turned to the back and was amazed by what he saw. A giant silvery parachute filled the entire screen.

Henry grinned proudly. 'A small gift from the CIA.'

Everyone sighed with relief and Milly pulled her hands away from her face.

'We actually made it,' Skye said as they slid through the open doors of the building and into a parking bay.

They came to a stop. Rory was the first one to snap open his seatbelt.

'That's it! I am NEVER going in the car if he's driving again,' Rory said, pointing at Henry. He pushed open the hatch, climbed through and stormed away. Milly, Skye and Jake all stared at Henry.

'What?' Henry protested. 'Did I not land safely?'

Their frowns deepened.

'You did give us a fright,' Skye said.

'I'm going for a shower to get this goo off,' Milly said.

'Me too. I stink,' Skye added.

Jake just shrugged at Henry and followed the girls.

'What smell? It's not that bad,' Henry called after Jake. 'Senses on.'

Jake turned back. Now that Henry had his senses switched back on, he could smell again. Covered in the stinky wax, he got one whiff of himself and then passed out.

The race teams sat in the cafeteria, chewing on their freeze-dried meals. Each team was at a separate table. Jake was used to getting his food from vending machines but he wasn't used to it being so quiet. Since Gradock had been arrested the remedial driving school had closed down. Now all that was left was a robotic vacuum cleaner that zipped back and forth, and it was the only other noise in the room besides the racers. Once again, Jake felt that the Blazing Comets were the outsiders. The other teams at least said hello to each other but Jake and his friends were treated like they were invisible. No-one seemed to pay them any attention.

Jake's thoughts drifted as he ate. He wondered why Henry had been sent by the CIA. Were they that worried the Comets would be badly beaten in the race? And even if that was the case, why did they care? They must have more important things to worry about.

A huge screen lit up on the cafeteria wall. A leaderboard was displayed in 3D. It looked so real that it seemed they could reach out and touch the numbers and letters.

'Oh wow!' Skye cried, clutching Jake's arm. 'We're in the lead!'

She was right. The Blazing Comets were in the top position.

'Ha! Pretty good for a bunch of wildcard kids,' Rory grinned.

Jake smiled back. Then he felt a hand land heavily on his shoulder. He was spun around in his seat and found himself looking into the very close-up face of one of the Misfits. It was the leader, Matt.

'Don't go getting too excited, Projectile Vomits,' Matt spat.

'It's the B-B-Blazing Comets,' Jake stammered.

Matt pulled him in close until Jake could just about taste the cafeteria goop on his breath. Jake gulped.

'That was just beginner's luck,' Matt said in a low growl. He pushed Jake back into his chair, spun him around and walked back to the Misfits, who were all snorting with laughter. When Jake finally stopped spinning and looked around dizzily, he caught the eye of Blake, the leader of the Neptune Goons. He was staring at Jake but when he noticed Jake catching him out, he quickly looked away.

'Are you all right?' Skye said.

'Ah … yeah, sure,' Jake said, trying to sound tougher than he felt.

He didn't like that Misfit one little bit. And right at that moment, Jake decided he was going to do everything he could to win the Rocket Battles for his team.

The face of one of the race organisers appeared on the screen in front of the leaderboard.

'Congratulations on reaching checkpoint one,' the announcer's voice boomed. 'The Venus Victors are out of the race, leaving

six teams. In approximately one minute you will be given your next clue. After that, there will be fifteen minutes to conduct all race car checks and prepare for take-off.' The screen went blank.

'I wonder where we'll be going next?' Skye said.

'Jup –' Henry began, 'ah, I mean, did anyone bring *jubes*?'

The clue flashed up on the screen. 'A storm is brewing. Red spot looming. Fifth in line, when there were once nine.'

Jake looked around. Some teams were busy scribbling notes, while others were gesturing as they argued about the destination. The Neptune Goons were the only ones who seemed to be taking more notice of the other teams than the Comets were, trying to figure out the clue. Jake noticed Blake glowering at the Misfits and, even though he didn't like them either, it made him feel strangely uncomfortable.

'Let's go do our checks,' Jake said.

Even though it was dim inside the hangar, the Comets' car was easy to find. It was not only because it was bright yellow but because it had two big dents, one on each side, from where the Mars Misfits had hit them. Jake looked at the dents. They were deep but not deep enough to cause any real damage. Then he noticed something odd. There was a paint mark in one of the dents where the Misfits had hit them. But the paint mark was purple, not red.

'Hey, Skye, look at this,' Jake said.

Skye looked at the purple mark and frowned.

'Shouldn't it be a red mark?' Jake wondered.

'It's probably from our car. It must have been purple before they painted it yellow for

the race,' Skye suggested.

Henry shrugged and walked about, tapping the car in different spots.

'No damage to engines. We are ready to go,' he said.

The team climbed inside the car and switched on the engines.

'From now on I'm driving and you can be *my* second-in-command,' Rory said to Henry, taking the driver's seat. Henry didn't argue.

Jake could hear the sound of the other teams' engines. Stage two of the battles was about to begin.

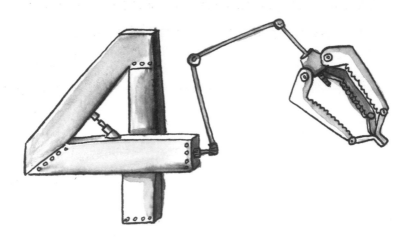

Skye was the one to figure out their next location. She knew Jupiter had the huge storm called the Great Red Spot, and that it was the fifth planet from the Sun. Jake was glad they had someone clever like Skye on board. The journey from the Moon to Jupiter was long and boring, though.

Jake brought up the forward projection screen but there wasn't much to see. Just lots of stars, endless rows of sparkles twinkling in

the sky. He began to feel sleepy and allowed himself to drift off ... until he woke with a start. Rory was braking, hard. Milly looked worried and was busily spinning dials and tapping buttons.

'What's going on?' Jake asked, trying to shake the fuzziness from his brain. How long had he been asleep?

The space car began to rattle. He stared at his screen. A green object plunged across the space in front of their car. He zoomed in with the viewfinder. 'The Pluto Pilgrims!' he cried.

The Pilgrims' green car went hurtling towards a huge gas planet and disappeared in a cloud of grey. Seconds later it shot back out again and went flying into space.

'They're out!' Milly cried.

'How did that happen?' Jake said.

'Simple,' Henry explained. 'The gravitational pull of Jupiter sucked the car in, then threw it back out again to land somewhere in outer space.'

'We have to pull back!' Rory cried.

'It's too strong,' Henry argued.

'The same thing's going to happen to us!' Milly said shakily.

Jake stared at the screen. All he could see was a swirling grey mist of gas.

'Switch to reverse,' Rory said.

Milly switched the car's controls over but the gas planet just got larger and larger as they were sucked in. *There has to be another way,* Jake thought. They had managed to slingshot to the Moon from Earth. Maybe they could do that with the even stronger pull of Jupiter.

'Accelerate!' Jake barked.

'No way! Unless you want to be pulverised into a pile of moon dust,' Rory cried.

'We can use gravity assist,' Jake said. 'Accelerate!'

Everyone looked at Jake like he'd been eating too many jubes.

'I'll show you.'

Rory moved over and let Jake take the controls as Milly switched the car over again. Jake accelerated hard. Just as he'd thought, the pull of Jupiter gave them even more speed and before long their car was being dragged along by the huge planet's gravity. They gained more and more speed.

They were coming in first yet again. *We might actually be able to win this race*, Jake thought. He moved over and let Rory take the controls again, then brought up the forward screen. He saw nothing.

'The Earth Avengers are right behind us,' Skye said.

Seconds later, she yelled out that the Mars Misfits had appeared too, and they were catching up to the Avengers.

They all turned nervously to look at the rear screen. The Mars Misfits hovered above the Avengers. Jake saw a hatch open up under the red car. A gigantic metal object was lowered from the hatch.

'What is that?' Milly cried.

'It looks like some kind of ... *claw*,' Skye said.

The giant claw moved lower and clamped down onto the Avengers' blue car, swinging it left, then right, then left again. Then it let go, tossing the car out into space. Jake watched the blue car flip, spin and vanish. The Misfits pulled the claw back into their car and kept flying towards the checkpoint.

'That was nasty,' Milly said.

Jake agreed but they had no time to think. They had to get to the next planet while they still had the supersonic speed from Jupiter – and while they could still get away from the

Misfits and their giant claw.

Then Jake saw the checkpoint. It was a huge ten-storey-high laser beam sign. The next clue shone from it: 'You're getting hotter but you're still not warm enough.'

'It's something about heat or temperature?' Rory said, puzzled.

'Honestly, it's easy,' Skye moaned, and announced at the same time as Milly: 'It's *our* planet!'

Of course! Jake thought. The next checkpoint was on Venus.

'I knew that,' Rory said, though no-one believed him.

They sailed through the checkpoint and Jake felt himself flying faster than he ever had before. The stars were just a blur of silver as they were thrown through the solar system. Finally they slowed as they headed into the atmosphere of Venus, careful to avoid lightning strikes shooting through its toxic clouds. This checkpoint proved the easiest to find of all, though. It glimmered with silver stardust on top of the tallest building on all of Venus.

The group slid down onto the shiny surface of the planet's landing platform.

'Activate the temperature control on your suits,' Milly instructed.

Jake felt a rush of cool air come over him as he adjusted the dial on his suit. The communication screen lit up as they released their seatbelts.

'Please make your way inside the main terminal for a meal break. You will have one hour until the next stage of the race begins.'

'One hour! Is that all?' Rory complained.

But one hour was more time than Jake wanted with the other teams around, especially the Mars Misfits.

5

LEADERBOARD

1. Blazing Comets
2. Mars Misfits
3. Saturn Speedsters
4. Neptune Goons

It was great to finally have some real food to eat. Fresh fruit and vegetables had been picked from the ecodome in one of Venus's super-modern floating cities. Yum! *It sure beats the freeze-dried stuff,* Jake thought. Sitting in the cafeteria was about as bad as he had expected, though. None of the other teams were happy the Blazing Comets were winning. The Comets ate in silence, heads down and not talking. Jake could feel the angry looks, especially from the Misfits' table. When they went up to get dessert the Misfits pushed in front.

'Vomits go last,' one of them said, pushing Jake in the shoulder.

As if things weren't bad enough already, the leaderboard was then displayed on the far wall. The Blazing Comets shone out like a star as the leading race team, followed by the Mars Misfits, the Saturn Speedsters and finally the Neptune Goons. Jake was amazed they were doing so well, but he was just as surprised that the Goons were coming last. It looked like this really was going to be the end of their racing career.

Jake scooped up a spoonful of ever-melting chocolate sauce, poured it on his refreeze ice-cream and looked at the board again. This time he saw two teams flashing on the screen – the Mars Misfits and the Neptune

Goons. Jake blinked as the two team placings swapped over so the Goons were in second place and the Misfits last. Then, just as quickly, they swapped back so the Misfits were second again.

'Did you see that?' Jake whispered.

'See what?' Rory asked.

'The Misfits and the Goons just changed position on the leaderboard.'

'Probably just a technical problem,' Rory shrugged.

'Mmm, yeah, probably,' Jake replied, as they sat down at a table to eat their dessert.

But Jake knew that technology hardly ever went wrong these days. He couldn't remember the last time he'd even seen a light go out on the space station. Still, he guessed it was possible. He looked over to the Goons. Blake was staring at the Misfits' table with a strange smirk on his face. *Did he see the switching on*

the screen too? Jake wondered.

Jake scooped up a mouthful of dessert but just as he was about to put it into his mouth, he ended up with a whole plateful. Not just in his mouth. The plate slid slowly down his face. Through the sticky mess he could see the ugly face of Matt the Misfit staring right at him. The three other members of his team were standing like a wall behind him.

'Keep winning this race and you'll end up looking worse than that, Vomit,' he snapped.

Jake went to stand but Skye gently pushed him back down again.

'Just ignore him,' she said.

'Yeah, just ignore me,' Matt sneered, 'it'll make it easier for us to knock you out of the race.'

The Misfit stuck out his hand and stabbed a spoon into Skye's bowl. He scooped some ice-cream and shoved it in his mouth. As he went to reach down again Henry grabbed onto

Matt's arm and in one movement had lifted him right off the ground. Matt spluttered and choked while Jake tried to cover a laugh. This was one time when having a cyborg as your friend was pretty good. Even Rory looked impressed.

'Put ... me ... down,' Matt croaked.

'You leave my friend alone,' Henry said slowly.

'Okay,' he stammered.

'And we are not the Projectile Vomits. We are the *Blazing Comets*. Got it?'

Matt nodded and Henry slowly returned him to the ground, still holding him tightly. When Henry finally let him go, Matt scampered back to his table to join his friends who had already run away.

'That was a bit mean, Henry,' Milly said.

'He was in need of some mind changing,' Henry said.

'I think you did that,' Rory laughed.

The leaderboard disappeared and an announcement was made: 'Take-off is in twenty minutes. Your next clue is: Small and rocky, I am hot. Bowl-shaped holes I have got.'

Jake's brain was feeling as mushy as his ice-cream so he said he'd do the race car checks while the others worked out the clue. He couldn't wait to get away from the Misfits too.

Jake entered the hangar where the race cars were parked. With the floating cities of Venus being such popular places to live, this area was much nicer and better lit than the one on the Moon. Everything was shiny and new, and there were all kinds of tools hanging from the walls, many that Jake had never even seen before. He quickly did all his checks on their car. It was still in pretty good shape, considering those dents. Then, as he pulled

a jack from the wall so he could lift the car to check underneath it, he heard a shuffling sound near one of the other cars.

Jake sneaked along the side wall of the hangar, carrying the jack over his shoulder like it was a bat. He heard the noise again and quickly hid behind the nearest car – the Saturn Speedsters'. He peered out from behind the car. The next one was the Neptune Goons' car. He caught a glimpse of a purple suit and a swish of golden hair. It was one of the Goons.

Jake sighed in relief and relaxed his arm. He was just about to go back to his car when he noticed something strange. There was a weird shimmering in the air around the Goons' car. It was like a red shadow. Jake took a step forward. He dropped the jack and it clanged to the floor noisily. The girl jumped and looked around. Jake crouched down, hidden, and the girl moved away quickly. The shimmering shadow disappeared.

Jake quietly returned the jack and sneaked back out of the hangar.

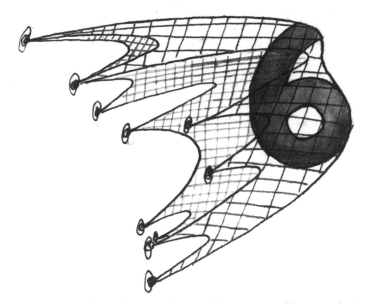

It hadn't taken Skye, Milly and Rory long to work out the clue. Only one planet was small and hot, and covered in craters. The next checkpoint had to be on Mercury. Just as they were heading back through the atmosphere of Venus, Jake felt a shudder through the whole car.

'What was that?' he cried.

Skye looked upset. 'We've just been hit by a lightning strike.'

49

Milly quickly checked the controls and engine function. 'It's all still working.'

Jake sighed in relief.

'Except ...'

'Except what?' he asked.

'It's taken out our boosters.'

Jake knew that was bad. Without the extra speed, they'd never be able to stay in the lead.

As they flew towards the small planet, Skye alerted them that the Saturn Speedsters had started catching up to them already. The Mars Misfits were not far behind them, with the Neptune Goons trailing along at the back. It was a close race by the time they could see Mercury. Jake yelled for Rory to accelerate. He was determined they would beat the other teams, especially the Misfits. No matter how hard Rory flew, though, without boosters the Saturn Speedsters soon overtook them. Then

the Mars Misfits zoomed past. That put the Comets back in third place, with only the Goons behind them.

Jake wondered how they were going to find the checkpoint. Even though Mercury was small compared to the other planets, finding that checkpoint was still like trying to find a speck of spacedust. He looked hard at the forward projection screen until the view went blurry. They flew around the planet but still couldn't find the checkpoint. They decided to head back in the opposite direction. Jake navigated so Rory could turn back around safely but he couldn't believe what he saw just moments later.

'We just passed the Misfits!' he exclaimed.

'That's good, isn't it?' Milly said.

'It would be, except we just turned around. We should have passed the Goons, not the Misfits.'

'Wow. We really must be going around in circles,' Milly said.

At that moment their car jerked to a stop. They were stuck in mid-air.

'What's going on?' Rory cried. 'The car won't move.'

'It's a net,' Skye said, looking through the rear screen. 'The Misfits have caught us in a gigantic net!'

Jake looked at the forward screen. It was covered with a crisscross pattern of thread.

'No problem,' Henry said calmly. 'I have a solution. One moment please.'

Everyone stared at the cyborg as he got Milly to press another button Jake had never noticed before. They heard a loud whirring sound.

'What are you doing?' Jake cried.

'Look!' Skye yelled.

Jake stared at the screen. Tiny whirling saws sprang from the outside of the car. The

blades cut through the net and they were free in less than a minute. Rory accelerated again.

'There's the checkpoint,' Jake cried.

Rory headed straight for it. He wasn't giving the Misfits a second chance at catching them.

Their next clue sent them to Neptune. They made it safely to the planet but the checkpoint was nowhere in sight.

'What now?' Milly asked.

'Whatever we do, we'd better work it out soon,' Skye said. 'We're starting to ice over.'

She was right. Silvery shards of ice were starting to creep over their bright yellow car. It was so cold compared to the inner planets they'd come from. Milly activated the heat generators to keep the car from icing over completely but soon the ice crept very slowly over the back of the car again. Just then Jake saw a flashing beacon.

'There's the checkpoint,' he cried and directed Rory towards it.

By the time they hit the checkpoint their car was almost completely iced over, and at that moment the communication screen came on. This time the leaderboard showed they were back in third place.

'Congratulations to all competitors on making it to Neptune. Your clue is: What goes around comes around. Good luck!' The screen went blank.

'What does that mean?' Milly yelled at the silent screen.

'What goes around comes around? It has to mean something round,' Skye suggested.

'That's a stupid clue. It doesn't tell us anything,' Rory complained.

'Henry, can you help us out?' Jake asked.

'That clue does not compute,' Henry said. 'I will need to think.'

He closed his cyborg eyes and moments later they flicked open again.

'I've got it,' he said.

'Well?' Milly asked.

'What goes *around* comes around,' Henry said. He made a fist with his right hand. Using his other hand, he drew a circle in the air around it.

'Oh! Rings. It's the rings of Saturn. That's where we have to go,' Skye said, excitedly.

Henry nodded and Milly started the launch sequence.

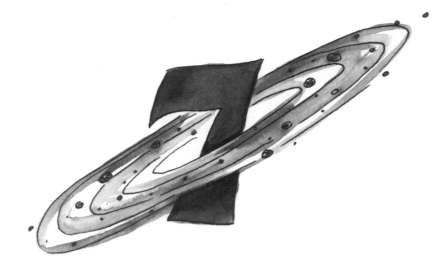

Even though they'd all learned about the rings of Saturn in school, seeing them in real life was totally different. Jake watched the rings as the car approached. Icy particles flew by, some as tiny as grains of rice, some as huge as space stations. The space car travelled so fast that many of the particles just looked like a blur going past. Rory pulled up and hovered at the far edge of the rings. Jake looked at the forward screen. It seemed the

Speedsters and the Misfits weren't sure which way to head either.

'What do we do now?' Milly wondered.

'We should go to the top of the planet and avoid the rings altogether,' Rory said.

'No,' Henry argued. 'We need to move into the rings to reach the next checkpoint.'

'We can't do that,' Rory said. 'We'll get wiped out for sure if we try flying through the rings.' Jake, Skye and Milly agreed with Henry, though. He always seemed to make the best decisions in the race.

'I can navigate you through,' Jake said.

Rory grumbled, taking the controls as Milly set the car into position. They were going in.

'Remind me whose great idea this was?' Rory complained a few minutes later.

The team ignored him. Asteroids moved at super-fast speeds all around them. If they

were hit with even the tiniest particle they would be blown to bits. Milly put up the safety shield screens around the car, but from here it was going to be up to their team driving skills to make it through.

Jake zoomed in on his screen. The Saturn Speedsters zipped past them. They were heading straight towards the orbiting rings. Then the Mars Misfits overtook them too and were just behind the Speedsters. Jake knew they were never going to win this race now their boosters were out, if they even survived the rings.

All five of them focused on navigating and looking out for asteroids. Jake could see the Saturn Speedsters heading in closer to the planet. He watched the screen carefully. The Speedsters just missed an asteroid. Jake zoomed in on their orange car and was just in time to see them nearly hit once again.

Then they were almost clipped on one side by another even larger asteroid, but still they kept moving towards the planet. Jake zoomed back out to wider vision.

'I hope they'll be okay,' Milly said.

'I hope *we'll* be okay,' Rory added.

'We have to gather more speed or we'll lose the race,' Jake said. He couldn't even see the Misfits and he still hadn't caught sight of the Goons either.

He watched the screen closely. 'Look out!' he cried, just before the image of an asteroid filled the screen.

Rory dipped sharply to the left, just missing it. Milly screamed. Then they were almost hit on the left side. Swerving quickly, Rory lost control and their car spun in circles in the air. He pulled back hard and righted the car just in time to miss the next incoming space particle. The Misfits then appeared from the right. They took the chance to get past the Speedsters, shooting back into the lead. The Comets pressed on, slowing as they battled to avoid asteroids. They were still in third position but Jake knew they'd be lucky to make it through the rings at all. He began to think they really were just wildcards – not real racers.

Then Jake saw a quick flash of something roaring past them. He thought they were about to be hit but saw a blaze of red on the screen. It was the Misfits, passing them. Jake frowned. That wasn't possible! The Misfits were already in the lead.

'The Misfits just came from *behind* us. But how?' Jake asked.

No-one seemed to have an answer. He turned back to the screen. 'Go left!' he shouted, just in time for Rory to avoid another asteroid.

Jake focused in on the Misfits. The

Speedsters were moving faster now and the two teams were almost touching shields. The Misfits shot sideways, banging into the other team's car.

'The Misfits are trying to knock the Speedsters into one of the asteroids,' Jake cried.

The Misfits zoomed back and forth in front of, and then behind, the Speedsters. Jake noticed something pale and golden that seemed to connect both cars.

'What's that?' he said.

Skye sprang up to the front and squinted at the screen.

'Whoa!' she gasped. 'They're lassoing the car.'

Jake zoomed in. Skye was right. Thin golden twine was wrapped around the Speedsters' car.

'What *is* that stuff?' Milly asked.

'It's spaceworm silk,' Henry said, 'the strongest silk in the solar system.'

'Oh, so you're finally deciding to join in this race?' Rory snapped.

'That's not nice,' Milly frowned.

'He's hardly helped at all. He's useless.'

'I am not allowed to drive with you in the car, according to my recent memory bank records. Remember?' Henry said.

'That doesn't mean you can't help out, second-in-command.'

'Quit arguing,' Skye interrupted. 'What are they going to do with the silk lasso?'

'I believe they are going to lasso them right out of orbit,' Henry stated.

The Misfits began to fly around and around the Speedsters, faster and faster. Once the lasso was wrapped tightly around the car, they released their end of the twine and the Speedsters' orange car went flying out of orbit and into deep space. The Speedsters were out of the race.

Shaken but still on course, the Blazing Comets continued to navigate through the rings of Saturn. When they had made it through the first ring they hovered to take a break. The communication screen lit up inside the car.

'Congratulations to the three remaining teams. Please check the leaderboard for results.'

The race results were displayed. Jake

couldn't believe it. The Neptune Goons were actually out in front this round, followed by the Comets and, finally, the Mars Misfits. *How is that possible?* Jake wondered. He hadn't even seen the Goons last round and it was the Misfits who had been in front of them. The screen flashed again, switching the Goons with the Misfits, but then changed back. It was the same thing that had happened when they saw the results on Venus, only this time the Goons were in the lead.

'This competition's rigged,' Rory complained. 'Either that or the Goons are cheating.'

'But how could they cheat?' Milly said.

'And where are they anyway?' Skye added. 'We haven't seen them since we arrived at Saturn.'

'Something's going on and you're not telling us, Henry,' Rory snapped. 'Why did the CIA send you?'

'Um, I don't think he's going to tell you anything,' Jake said.

'Why not? We need to know,' Rory argued.

Jake pointed at Henry. Rory looked over.

'He's shut himself down,' Jake said.

'He's done it just to get out of telling us anything,' Rory grumbled. 'Let's just switch him back on.'

'I would agree with you,' Jake said, peering at the control panel on Henry's arm, 'but he's only on two per cent power. I think he's going to have to charge up his battery first.'

'Wait! The Misfits are coming up behind us,' Skye said.

'But how can they be *behind* us?' Jake said.

'I don't know but it's time to get moving,' Skye replied.

Rory accelerated hard and they rocketed on towards the second ring of Saturn.

The next ring wasn't too hard to get through now they were used to avoiding the asteroids. Though the particles seemed to move a little faster, they still got through okay. But when they saw the third ring, Jake wasn't so confident. This one was so much denser. There were asteroids of all shapes and sizes moving around so fast that the ring looked like a solid piece of ice in front of them. It would be almost impossible to navigate Rory through it.

'There's no way we can fly through there,' Rory cried.

'We have to follow the other teams or we'll lose the race,' Skye said.

Jake knew both of them were right but what was the answer? They needed to at least keep up but he didn't want to be pulverised either. He turned to Henry. He was now at seventy per cent power. *That should be enough,* Jake

thought. He switched him on.

'Yes? What did I miss? Where are we?' Henry said.

'The third ring of Saturn,' Milly said.

'What? What are we still doing in the rings of Saturn? We'll never make it!'

That wasn't exactly what Jake had expected him to say.

'Calm down, Henry,' Rory said.

'We have to get out of here,' Henry cried.

'What about the race?' Milly said.

'We can still win,' Henry replied.

'You're the one who told us to go into the rings,' Rory argued. 'We made it this far already, and I'm not losing the race because you're scared.'

'I am not scared,' Henry insisted.

'Then we're going in.'

'But the checkpoint was meant to be at the second ring and ...' He suddenly stopped talking.

'Ha! I knew you were hiding something,' Rory said.

'Come on Henry, spill the beans,' Jake added.

'Beans? What beans?' he said.

'Tell us why you're here and what you know about the race,' Jake said firmly.

'One moment please,' Henry responded.

The cyborg opened up his arm and quickly started typing a series of numbers on the panel inside it. Finally he stopped and looked up.

'Oh no! It seems my calculations were incorrect,' he cried. 'We have to go to the top of the planet.'

'That's what I said we should do when we first got to Saturn,' Rory groaned and rolled his eyes. 'No-one *ever* listens to me.'

On Henry's command, Milly moved the car into a vertical position.

'This is never going to work!' Rory exclaimed.

'I have activated the emergency back-up boosters. It will work perfectly,' Henry said.

'We have back-up boosters now?' Rory scolded. 'You could have told us that earlier.'

Henry ignored him as Milly switched into overdrive.

Rory followed Henry's directions and headed towards the top of the planet, even though he wasn't happy about it. Jake felt his whole body press against the back of the seat so hard that it felt like his belly button was poking out of his back. He pushed his arms forward. It was like he was pressing against a brick wall even though there was just air in front of him. He used all his strength to reach forward and switch on the projection screen. Asteroids were shooting straight towards them. It looked like a sky full of falling stars. They took off, heading up through the ring.

'Left. Right. Right. *Left!*' Jake ordered.

As Rory flew around the flying particles Jake began to think they had no chance of surviving this race. Milly was so scared she covered her eyes the whole time. Even Skye looked pale.

'Right. Right. Left. Left. Hard right,' Jake

barked, directing Rory as more and more particles flew towards the screen.

Luckily, their team driving skills meant that before long they were free of the rings. Milly righted the car and Rory flew across the top of the brown, gassy surface of Saturn.

'You may release the firm grip on your seat now, Rory, and decelerate,' Henry said. 'We have safely arrived at the top of planet Saturn.'

'Good one!' Rory snapped. 'You might know more about the race than us but we're probably out of it now because you messed up.'

Jake hated to admit it but he thought Rory was right. The girls looked like they agreed too since they both looked disappointed. If Henry had let them know everything they might have figured it out sooner.

They all started talking about where the checkpoint could be and how they were going to find it. Then Jake noticed Henry fumbling around under the seats. When he came back up again he was holding a strange-looking backpack. It was silver and shiny and it looked soft to the touch, like it was filled with nothing but air. They all looked at Henry as he put the straps over his shoulders.

'What are you doing?' Jake cried.

'The CIA has just alerted me that my mission is about to commence,' he said.

'Alert?' Rory said. 'What alert?'

Henry held up his arm. His watch was flashing blue. 'I have fifteen minutes until commencement.'

Jake was annoyed. He had always sided with Henry but now he knew Rory had been right. All Henry cared about was his CIA mission. He didn't care if they won the race after all. Everyone else looked just as angry as Jake felt.

'So you brought us up here just for your

mission, not to find the checkpoint?' Jake yelled.

'Don't worry. The checkpoint will appear soon too. You just have to let them know you are here.'

'What does that mean? You're not even making any sense,' Jake snapped.

'Sorry, I must power down. I need full energy for the mission.'

With that, Henry shut himself down again.

'Oh no you don't,' Jake said.

He went to switch Henry back on again so the cyborg could give them an explanation but Henry had locked his controls.

The next fifteen minutes passed slowly. They were all tired and cranky. They hadn't had any rest since they'd left Venus.

'I wish we had something to eat,' Rory complained.

As if by magic a console on the front

dashboard of the car opened. Inside were four space meals.

'Wow! How did you do that?' Milly asked.

'I don't know,' Rory admitted.

No-one cared. They were so hungry they each grabbed a meal and scoffed it down quickly. As they were finishing the food, Skye switched on her screen.

She gasped.

'It's the Mars Misfits,' she shouted.

Everyone peered at the screen. She was right. The Misfits were shooting up through the rings. Milly shrieked. Henry switched himself back on.

'Yes? What's happening?' he said.

Everyone just ignored him. They were still angry, especially now it looked like the Misfits were sure to beat them.

'It is time to begin the mission,' Henry said. He placed himself in the emergency exit seat.

The four Comets glared at him.

'You could tell us what you're doing before you abandon ship,' Jake said.

'I was sent to stop the Misfits before they carry out their plan to destroy Mars.'

'*What*?' they all cried at once.

'All I know is the Misfits plan to blow up Mars,' Henry said as he tightened his backpack.

'That's *all*?' Rory exclaimed. 'That's my planet you're talking about!'

'Sorry, time for departure!' Henry replied.

He pressed the exit button. Rory went to grab Henry but he was ejected from the space car before Rory could reach him.

Henry shot down towards Saturn's rings, a human torpedo. Well, a half-human one. Everyone was silent as they watched him. Not only had they just been told the Mars Misfits were planning to destroy Rory's home planet but now Henry seemed to be on a mission to get himself killed. Jake saw Henry fly down towards the Misfits, his arms pressed firmly to his sides as he weaved between ice particles. Some

came so close Jake thought he was going to be struck for sure. It was only when he started to feel dizzy that he realised he'd been holding his breath. Just then Jake saw an asteroid hit Henry along one side of his body. He slowed for a moment but then kept going. That was a close one!

Rory's eyes were rounder than planets as he leaned over and stared at the screen. Jake knew how scared and worried he must be. He had felt the same way when he thought his own home planet, Earth, was going to be destroyed by the evil Gradock. What Jake couldn't understand was why the Misfits would want to destroy their own planet.

Jake watched on the screen as Henry got closer to the Misfits. And closer. He was coming up fast and he was still gaining speed as he spiralled downward. If he hit the red space car at that speed he'd be splattered like a space bug on a windscreen when he landed. But just as it looked like he was going to smash headfirst into the Misfits' car, Henry pulled the cords on his backpack and a big mushroom shape covered his body. He'd opened a parachute and landed safely.

Phew, Jake thought. *But what is he going to do now?*

Before Jake could even guess he saw something incredible. A *second* Mars Misfits car was coming up beside the one Henry was headed towards. There were now two identical red cars, side by side. How was that possible?

Jake looked at the forward projection screen again. Both cars were still there. He zoomed in on the first car and watched as Henry opened the hatch on top of the car and disappeared inside. Jake zoomed out. The two cars were still there. He rubbed his eyes but the screen still showed both of them.

'Take a look at this,' Jake exclaimed, pointing.

'Someone tell me I'm not seeing double,' Rory cried.

'You're not – there are two cars,' Jake said.

'That explains how the Misfits have been winning the space races. There are two of them,' Skye said. 'Why hasn't anyone noticed this before?'

That's true, Jake thought. *Someone would have noticed.* Then he realised something. They hadn't seen the Goons in ages. Why did they always seem to disappear when the Mars Misfits appeared? Could the Goons somehow be disguised as the Mars Misfits? He thought back to how he'd seen the strange red shimmering around the Goons' car in the hangar on Venus. Maybe that had something to do with it. Maybe he hadn't imagined that red shadow after all. And then there was the purple paint mark left on their car. Could it have really been the Goons that had hit them?

Jake told the others what he thought was going on. Even though it seemed impossible, there was no other way to explain it. The Goons *had* to be somehow disguising themselves as the Misfits.

'We have to warn Henry,' Skye said.

'There's no way of contacting him. It's up to us,' Jake said.

'I wish he was here,' Milly said. 'He'd know what to do.'

'If you're right, and the Goons are disguising themselves as the Misfits, which red car belongs to the real Misfits and which is really the Goons?' Rory asked.

'And which team are the real baddies?' Milly added.

'What did you just say?' Jake said.

Milly frowned. 'If they both look the same,

we don't know which is which, do we?'

Jake made a split-second decision. 'Suit me up!' he demanded.

The others all looked at him, shocked. But Jake knew exactly what he needed to do.

Even though there was a fifty per cent chance that Henry had gone after the real Misfits, there was just as much chance he had accidentally headed for the Goons, who looked like the Misfits. Either way, Jake had to make sure they had both cars covered. Rory handed Jake a space suit.

'Have you gone completely space mad?' Skye shrieked. 'You're going to get yourself killed! If you don't get hit by an asteroid, you'll get caught by the Misfits – or by the Goons, I mean.'

'I have to go in,' Jake replied. 'If Henry's in the wrong car it could be too late for him to stop Mars being blown to bits.'

'He's right,' Rory agreed. 'There's no time to

waste. My whole planet could be destroyed.'

'Then I'm coming with you, Jake,' Skye said.

Jake knew there was no point arguing, especially since Skye was already pulling on her space suit. Plus, she looked more determined about going than someone trying to catch the last space jube.

They entered the airlock chamber together and Jake gave the signal for Rory to send them out into space.

If Jake had thought navigating ice particles was scary from inside a space car, then going in as a human torpedo was light years more terrifying. He had to keep hyper-alert as the asteroids whizzed past him. He ducked and weaved, turning his body one way and then the other. Every now and then he caught a glimpse of Skye. She was also twisting this way and that, swerving much better than he was. *How does*

she do that? Jake wondered. She made it look easy while sweat was dripping off him like an ice-block left in the sun. He was sure he would be blown into a million tiny pieces before he even made it to the second red car.

In the next instant he saw it coming up fast. Jake stretched his arms out in front of him, like he was Superman. He was ready to land on top of the space car. He reached it and braced himself for impact. Only he didn't hit the car. He travelled straight through it.

There was nothing there.

Now Jake knew how there had been two Mars Misfits cars. The second car was just a hologram! The red glow he had seen around the car when he'd caught the Goon girl in the hangar was a holographic image. It wasn't the Misfits at all – it was just the Goons in disguise. *So that's how the Goons appeared and disappeared!*

Below him he could now see the real Goons' purple car. It was coming up quickly. Again, he prepared to land. What he wasn't ready for was how fast he was going, which meant he hit the car – hard. Jake landed ungracefully on his stomach, the wind knocked out of him. He took in a huge breath of the oxygen from his suit, then started choking and coughing.

Just as he'd finally got his breath back, something landed smack on his back. The air was pushed out of his lungs again. At first he thought he must have been hit by an asteroid. Whatever it was slid off and landed beside him. He turned his head to see Skye. Even through her space suit he could see she had turned redder than Mars. He wasn't the only one embarrassed about the messy landing. Then she pointed towards the car's entry hatch and Jake nodded. They were going in.

Jake quickly realised landing on the Goons' car without a plan wasn't such a great idea. They hadn't figured anything out except that they had to get into the car. Now he and Skye had gone inside they didn't know what to do. The only helpful thing was that the Goons had somehow created a normal gravity field in the car and at least they weren't floating about all over the place.

The car looked like it had been pretty amazing in its day. There were all kinds of dials and controls Jake had never seen before. The seats reclined and even had cup holders and suction trays. The walls were covered in projection screens so it was like looking out a normal window, only the Goons could zoom in and out by voice command. But now everything looked old and worn. Some of the controls had come out and were hanging on by wires. Even the floor was dirty and stained. And now three Goons had swivelled their faded chairs around and were staring at him and Skye. One of them was the girl that Jake had seen in the hangar on Venus.

'Um, hi!' Jake said weakly.

'So, you managed to figure out our plan, hey?' the leader, Blake, said in a snaky voice.

'We did go flying straight through your hologram,' Skye said, crossing her arms.

Even though they were in really big trouble Jake couldn't help but grin. Skye was so calm,

even now.

'Yes, a clever trick of ours, don't you think?' Blake replied.

'How did you do it?' Skye asked.

'Easy. We just took an image of the Misfits' car and put up a projection shield. When we wanted to look like the Misfits we switched the image projection on and when we wanted to be the Goons we switched it off.'

Blake pressed a lever on his chair and it actually moved forward, floating towards Jake. 'Since you're here you can help us!' Blake sneered.

'I don't think that's such a great idea, Blake,' said a taller and skinnier Goon in a tiny, squeaky voice. He also moved his chair closer to Jake and Skye.

'And why not, Eric?' Blake snapped.

'Um, well, um, er, because then they'll know our plans,' Eric stammered.

Blake roared with laughter, his whole body shaking. Jake and Skye just looked at each other. This lot was completely space-bug crazy.

'Who are they going to tell?' Blake said, tears streaming down his face from laughter.

He did have a pretty good point. Now they were here there wasn't much they could do. They were stuck. But there was one thing Jake knew for sure: 'If you think we're going to help you win this race, you can forget it,' he said.

'Who said anything about helping us win?' Blake replied.

'Yeah,' Eric agreed. Then he turned to Blake. 'Um, er, why not?'

'Because, space brain, we're not trying to win, we're trying to destroy the planet that keeps on beating us every year. That way we will always be the champions,' Blake barked.

The two kept arguing about how they were

going to ruin the Mars Misfits and blow up Mars to make sure they were the winners from now on. Jake had to figure out a way to stop them. And fast.

'Um, excuse me,' Jake interrupted.

'Hand up if you want to ask a question,' Blake said, snorting at his own joke.

'How exactly do you think ...' Jake began.

'Uh-uh. Hand *up*,' Blake said, snorting again.

Jake felt stupid but he put his hand up.

'Yes?' Blake said.

'How exactly do you think you're going to blow up an entire planet from a space car?'

'Shall we show them, Lucy?' Blake said, gesturing to the third Goon who was sitting by the controls.

Lucy nodded. Jake remembered the shimmering shadow he had seen around the Goons' car on Venus, and the way Lucy had run away from the hangar. She had to be the mastermind behind the technology they'd used to disguise themselves.

'Then let's begin,' Blake said.

Lucy then brought up the rear projection screen. All Jake could see was a swirling current of asteroids. He still couldn't imagine what the Goons had planned. He could only hope they weren't clever enough to put their plan into action. Blake and Eric seemed to be about as smart as a couple of space bacteria. But then he heard a metallic click and he turned to see Lucy pressing buttons on the control panel.

'Missile number one is ready for release,' she announced.

Jake couldn't help himself. He started laughing.

'You think this is funny, Vomit?' Blake sneered.

'You can't blow up a whole planet with one missile!'

'How about six?' Lucy said.

'Not even –' Jake began.

'Six missile-powered asteroids.'

Jake's smile quickly faded. If one asteroid hitting Earth could wipe out the dinosaurs, then six missile-powered ones were sure to destroy the whole planet of Mars. He looked over at Skye. When he saw how worried she looked he knew it must be possible.

'Now we just need a big enough asteroid and we can attach the first missile to it,' Blake said, rubbing his hands together.

'Oooh, there's one, there's one,' Eric cried, pointing to the screen like an excited little kid.

Lucy entered some numbers on the computer.

'Okay ... and ... we're ready to let missile one fly.'

Blake hit the release button. Jake stared at the projection screen helplessly as the missile shot from underneath the car and headed straight towards the asteroid Eric had pointed out. The missile landed and attached itself to the huge icy piece of rock. Jake heard Skye gasp. Her hands covered her mouth and her eyes were wide with fright.

'Why are you doing this?' Jake demanded.

'You've never been famous so you wouldn't understand,' Blake said.

'Yeah,' Eric added, 'we used to have everything we could ever want. Money, cool cars, nice clothes. And best of all, everyone loved us.'

'But not anymore,' Lucy added. 'No-one even knows who the Goons are now. And we want that all back. Don't we, boys?'

'But ... but ... think of all the people who live on Mars,' Jake stammered.

'We have. That's why we're going to make sure there's never another team as fast as the Misfits. Destroy the planet, destroy the competition,' Blake argued.

'Best of all, no-one will ever know it was us. With our disguise, everyone will think the Misfits destroyed their own planet, and we'll be the champions again,' Eric added, grinning.

'But my friend, Rory ...' Jake began.

The Goons ignored him as they happily pointed out other large asteroids, then released the remaining five missiles. Each one attached itself to a giant asteroid. Worst of all, Jake knew there was nothing they could do to stop them because they were stuck on board with the Goons, and no-one but the Blazing Comets even knew of the team's evil plans.

'Now we just have to set the missiles' course for Mars and the planet is doomed.' The Goons laughed nastily together. Jake watched helplessly and saw that Skye had turned whiter than the Moon.

He thought hard. They *had* to stop the Goons from sending the missiles to Mars. He wished Henry was with them. He'd be able to reprogram the missiles' course. But Jake knew nothing about programs and even if he did he could never overpower the Goons. It was three against two and they were all bigger than him and Skye.

If only he could alert the other cars somehow! But even if he could communicate with them, would the Mars Misfits even listen? Matt had made it pretty clear that he didn't like the Comets being chosen as the wildcard entry in the race one little bit, and he especially didn't like Jake. What chance did Jake have of getting someone who had pushed a plate in his face to help? If only the Misfits knew their own planet was under threat …

'The course is set. Now, all we have to do is hit the final command button,' Blake said.

'I'll do it!' Eric said, rubbing his hands together in glee.

Jake knew that once Eric hit that button there would be no stopping the missiles from heading straight to Mars. He ran his fingers through his hair, feeling helpless.

But as he felt his hair, still sticky with wax, he had an idea.

While the Goons were busy watching the asteroids on the screen he slowly reached into his pocket. He gave Skye a nudge and showed her the jar of no-gravity hair wax.

Jake whispered, 'You distract them for a minute and I'll let the wax loose.'

Skye smiled and nodded. She took a deep breath, pointed to the rear projection screen and screamed, 'Oh no! WHAT'S THAT?'

The Goons all turned and zoomed over in their hovering chairs. Meanwhile, Jake tipped the jar into his hand until all the hair wax came out, holding his breath so he didn't have to smell the foul stuff. He quickly smeared the gooey, stinky wax over the controls, plugging them up. He glanced over at the Goons. They had no idea what he'd just done but it wouldn't be long before they figured it out. Now there was just one thing left to do.

Jake knew that if the race organisers could make announcements through the cars, there must be a way for them to get messages out too. He fumbled over the maze of controls and dials, now sticky with hair goo. Then he found a small black microphone hanging off the side of the driver's console. He pulled it out and switched it on. He hoped this would work. The Goons were still staring at the rear screen, trying to figure out what

Skye was screaming about. She was a good actor, that was for sure, and Jake started to think the plan might actually work. He held down the black button on the microphone. Then he saw Blake scrunch his nose up in disgust.

'Yuck, Eric, what did I tell you about eating space cabbage during the race?'

'It wasn't me,' Eric argued. 'Lucy must be the one who farted.'

'I don't fart,' Lucy cried, blushing even though it hadn't been her.

'Then it must have been one of those horrible Vomits.'

Jake knew he had only seconds until the Goons caught them out. He spoke into the microphone. He just hoped they could hear him in the other cars.

'It's me, Jake. We're with the Goons. They're the ones who've been doing the race sabotage.

 98

They're going to blow up Mars. There are six asteroids with missiles attached. We have to stop them before they activate the missiles' course.'

The microphone crackled and Jake heard Rory's voice, 'Copy that. Henry has already alerted us.'

Then there was a clicking sound and Henry's voice came through. 'I knew it wasn't the Misfits when I entered their car. Now that the Misfits know their planet is under threat they will help. I can use my computer panel to divert the missiles from Mars but we will still need to stop –'

Before he could say anything else Blake took hold of the microphone and ripped it straight out of the control panel. He tossed it aside, angrily.

'I knew you were up to something. But it's too late. You'll never stop us now.'

The Goons followed the smell, sniffing around until they found where it was coming from. Blake gasped when he saw the terminal covered in the stinky, sticky wax.

'ERIC!' he yelled, even though Eric was just beside him. 'GET THIS STUFF OFF – NOW!'

Eric pulled a scrunched-up handkerchief from his pocket and started wiping down the terminal.

'Not with that, you moon amoeba. You need to scrape it off!'

Lucy pulled out something that looked like a cross between a shovel and a potato peeler. She quickly worked to scrape off the wax, trying to hold her breath as she did.

As Lucy worked on the wax, Jake looked for the Misfits and the Comets. But there was nothing. No matter how hard he stared at the projection screens, all he could see were asteroids whizzing by and the shine

of a billion stars. Soon the course would be activated, sending the missiles towards Mars. The other cars had to hurry, especially now Lucy had the hair wax off the controls. They were already running out of time.

'It's ready.'

Lucy hit the final command button. A tone sounded through the space car. The missiles were heading to Mars. It was too late. Jake knew there was no way they would be able to stop the missiles without the help of the others now. The only way to save the planet would be to somehow push the missiles off course.

Just then he heard a clunk coming from under the Goons' car. The whole car shook and Skye knocked into Jake. Could it be Henry or the Comets?

'What was that?' Eric exclaimed.

Thinking quickly, Skye said, 'Someone's

trying to attack. You'd better go down and check it out.'

Eric's eyes grew rounder than a full moon.

'Yeah, get down there and see what's going on,' Blake sneered.

'There could be more than one of them. There are four Misfits, if it's them,' Jake added.

'The Vomit is right,' Blake said. 'We all have to go. Come on!'

Skye winked at Jake as he watched Lucy enter the airlock chamber with Blake and Eric. She pressed a big button with a key drawn on it, locking them in.

Skye and Jake raced into action. It was time to put a serious stop to the missiles. While they quickly tried to make sense of the Goons' control panels, they saw the Comets' yellow car appear on the forward screen. Just as Jake had thought, the clunk *had* come from another car! It was a clever decoy, bumping the Goons' car from below, Jake thought. Then they saw the red Misfits join the yellow Comets on the screen. He started to think maybe they could stop those asteroids after all, especially if Henry could change the missiles' course in time.

The Blazing Comets and the Misfits shot forward and the Goons, with Skye in the driver's seat, followed closely behind. All three cars were going to have to reach maximum speed if they were to stop the missiles before they reached Mars.

Skye lined up the Goons' car beside the first missile-loaded asteroid. She made a hard left turn and slammed straight into it. Jake felt the car shudder with the impact but the missile

just kept going. They needed a stronger car, Jake thought, but that wasn't going to appear any time soon. He knew one thing might help, and he scanned the control panel until he found it. He pressed a button and the safety shield covered the car.

Skye gave him the thumbs-up sign and they lined the car up again. This time she slammed the asteroid side on. It worked. It went flying off course and into deep space. That was one down, five to go.

The communication screen lit up. 'The clue for the next destination is: The red planet, that is right. A space suit you will wear tonight.'

'I can't believe it. The finish line is on Mars,' Skye exclaimed.

'If it still exists,' Jake added. He saw another missile whiz across the screen. The Comets had thrown the second one off course, but Jake could see the whole back of the Comets' car was smashed in. It was slowing down and wouldn't make it to any of the other missiles now.

Jake saw the Misfits hit a third missile. It spun, flew off course and disappeared. A thick cloud of smoke appeared. It was coming out of the back of the Misfits' car and they started losing speed too. There were three missiles still to go but now they were fast approaching Mars and the red planet loomed before them.

Skye slammed into another missile, sending that one off course as well.

Now there were only two missiles left, but with the other cars out of action there was no way Skye and Jake could stop them both in time. Skye accelerated after the asteroids but they couldn't even catch up to one, let alone two. The only chance they had of saving Mars was Henry. Could he stop them in time?

Jake and Skye looked at each other in

silence. Jake closed his eyes. In just a few seconds it would be too late to save Mars.

But when he opened his eyes again he saw something amazing on his screen. The two asteroids had just stopped in mid-air. It happened so quickly that Skye almost crashed straight into one. Then the huge rocks turned and shot away so fast Jake could hardly see them. In the far distance a small flame appeared as one missile exploded, then another. Henry must have figured out how to change the missiles' course. He had done it. Mars was saved! Jake clapped his hands.

'Jake! We have a problem!' Skye yelled.

Jake looked at his screen. Skye was right. The screen was bright red. They were about to hit Mars. Skye pulled back as hard as she could but they were coming up too fast. Jake saw the landing strip. As they got closer and closer, he saw a crowd of people waving flags and cheering. They were at the finish line of the space race to watch the winners fly in. The only problem was that no-one would know their car was out of control. There was a lake next to the runway. Jake knew it was their only chance of coming in safely and not landing on top of the cheering crowd.

'Go left!' Jake screamed.

Skye turned hard. Seconds later, the battered car hit the lake and slid across the surface, floating on the water. Jake and Skye looked at each other. Jake was amazed they were still alive.

'Good driving,' Jake said.

Skye laughed and then pressed the exit hatch.

Jake was the first to poke his head out. People were wading into the water, cheering as they went. Before he knew it he'd been bundled

across to the shore where a heavy medal was hung over his head. A shiny ticket was put in his hand. Jake looked at it. He couldn't believe it. They had actually *won* the Rocket Battles, and this year's prize was tickets to the Robot Games! It was nearly impossible to get tickets to the Games. It was the most famous event in the solar system. He looked over at Skye in amazement.

Then he thought of the others. He knew both cars had been in trouble. He looked up to the sky to see if they were coming in. They weren't anywhere to be seen.

Then, above the roar of the crowd, he heard a rattling engine. A speck of red appeared and the Misfits came in to land, smoke pouring out of the back of their car. Moments after the yellow Comets came into view and clattered in to land too.

Squeezing through the crowd, Jake and Skye

reached their friends. They laughed as Rory and Milly were given their winning medals and tickets as well. They were the winning team because Jake and Skye had been the first to cross the finish line. If only the crowd knew they'd not only won the race but had saved the planet as well. Finally, Henry came out of the Misfits' car and was given a medal too.

When he looked over Jake saw the Misfits were standing in a small group, alone, their arms crossed hard across their space-suited chests. Jake nudged Skye and the other Comets followed his gaze. Jake walked over to the Misfits, not sure what to say. They had been race champions for so long they were sure to be angry the Comets had won, especially with them being the wildcards.

'So, Vomit, guess we're pretty glad you saved our planet,' Matt said. To Jake's surprise, all three Misfits broke into huge smiles.

'Thanks,' he answered, shaking Matt's hand. 'It's lucky you believed me when I sent the message. We couldn't have done it without your team. How did you know I was telling the truth?'

'That was easy,' Matt explained. 'We already knew something was wrong when we saw the leaderboard changing our position all the time.'

'Yeah,' another explained, 'and when Henry started telling us how horrible we were with our space sabotage tricks we *really* knew something was wrong. We might be good at sabotage but we'd never put other drivers in any real danger. That was all the work of the Goons.'

The third Misfit cut in. 'Then your message came through and it all made sense. The Goons had been pretending to be us.'

Two CIA agents, Bree and Will, appeared

from the crowd. They waved at Jake and his friends.

'I have to go,' Jake said.

'See you in next year's race, Vomit,' Matt said. 'There's always next time to beat you.'

Jake smiled and ran to catch up with the others. Henry was standing beside Bree and Will when they got over to them.

'Well done, team. The CIA couldn't have done it without you,' Will said.

'Yes, sorry we couldn't tell you about the mission,' Bree added. 'We had to be sure you looked like you were just part of the race.'

'Only Henry was to know the race checkpoints so he could carry out the mission,' Will explained.

Rory's face turned bright red as he looked at Henry. 'So you did know all along?'

'Um, yes. The CIA alerted me that some of their missiles had been stolen and tracked to

the space race headquarters. I thought it was the Misfits,' Henry added.

'We *all* thought it was the Misfits,' Bree explained.

'But it was you kids who figured out it was really the Goons,' Will added.

'The Goons!' Jake remembered. 'They're still inside the airlock chamber of their car!'

'Good. It should be easy to arrest them then,' Will said. 'Let's go, Bree.'

'Thanks again, Blazing Comets,' Bree said, and followed Will towards the lake.

Just as Rory was about to strangle Henry for not telling them about the CIA mission, a 3D camera appeared in their faces. Rory quickly dropped his hands into a hug instead and smiled for the camera. Jake was handed a moving trophy of a revolving space car and all he could see for the next few minutes was the bright flash of cameras going off. It was so weird that everyone was celebrating their win when they had no idea the planet they stood on had come so close to being destroyed forever. Jake smiled at Skye. She smiled back.

Then Jake's mum raced over. She bent down and gave him a big sloppy kiss on the cheek. When he pulled away he saw tears were streaming down her face.

'Oh, thank goodness you're all right,' she sobbed. 'I knew your father should never have let you go in that race.'

'Ah, excuse me, but it was you who agreed he could go in it,' Dad answered.

'Only because I knew he could win it,' Mum replied.

Jake just smiled at his parents. 'Um, I'll be back in a minute.' He left his mum and dad arguing and joined his friends.

In the distance, over the lake, they watched the Goons being taken away in space cuffs by

the CIA.

'Guess they won't be trying to destroy planets any time soon,' Jake said.

'No, and now we've just got the Robot Games to look forward to,' Skye added.

'I can't wait!' Rory said.

'I'm glad we won't be having any adventures for a while,' Milly said, grinning. 'Right, Henry?' Henry just smiled in return.

Jake's mum and dad pulled up in the family's space car.

'Guess I'd better get going,' Jake said.

They all said goodbye and Jake climbed into the car, happy to be a passenger again.

'Let's go home,' he said to his parents.

ABOUT THE AUTHOR

Candice's quirky style, fast-paced narratives and originality appeals to reluctant boy readers in particular.

Following several years working in the media, Candice now devotes her time to her writing and to raising her two young daughters. She is also a Literacy Champion for the Municipal Literacy Partnership Program (MLPP).